What's the Matter With A.J.?

by Dr. Lawrence Balter

UNDERSTANDING JEALOUSY

Illustrated by Roz Schanzer

BARRON'S

New York • London • Toronto • Sydney

All inquiries should be addressed to:
Barron's Educational Series, Inc.
250 Wireless Boulevard
Hauppauge, NY 11788

International Standard Book No. 0-8120-6119-5

Library of Congress Catalog No. 89-6650

Library of Congress Cataloging-in-Publication Data

Balter, Lawrence.
    What's the matter with A.J.?

    (Stepping stone stories)
    Summary: The arrival of a new baby in the family affects an older
child, who responds with jealousy and unpredictable outbursts of
anger. Includes a discussion of this problem for parents and teachers.
    [1. Babies—Fiction. 2. Brothers and sisters—Fiction] I. Schanzer,
Rosalyn, ill.   II. Title
III Series.
PZ7.B2139Wh 1989   [E]   89-6650
ISBN 0-8120-6119-5

PRINTED IN HONG KONG

9012   4900   987654321

Dear Parents and Teachers:

The books in this series were written to help young children better understand their own feelings and the feelings of others. It is hoped that by hearing these stories, or by reading them, children will see that they are not alone with their worries. They should also learn that there are constructive ways to deal with potentially disrupting circumstances.

All too often children's feelings are brushed aside by adults. Sometimes, because we want to protect youngsters and keep them happy, we inadvertently trivialize their concerns. But it is essential that we identify their emotions and understand their concerns before setting out to change things.

Children, of course, are more likely to act on their feelings than to reflect on them. After all, reflection requires tolerance that, in turn, calls for a degree of maturity. A first step, however, is learning to label and to talk about one's feelings.

I also hope to convey to parents and others who care for children that while some of a child's reactions may be troublesome, in all likelihood they are the normal by-products of some difficult situation with which the child is trying to cope. This is why children deserve our loving and patient guidance during their often painful and confusing journey toward adulthood.

Obviously, books can do only so much toward promoting self-understanding and problem-solving. I hope these stories will provide at least a helpful point of departure.

Lawrence Balter, Ph. D.

On a Wednesday morning not too terribly long ago in the town of Crescent Canyon it was breakfast time.

"Feed me," A.J. Brown ordered.
"Oh, come on. You're a big boy and you can feed yourself," answered his mother. "Hurry up now or you'll be late for nursery school. Jenny's mom will be here to drive you any minute."

A.J. scowled.

"If I'm such a big boy," he muttered under his breath, "how come I can't just drive myself to school?"

But his mother was too busy with the baby to hear.

A.J. sloshed some cereal around.

He was just about to pour a little orange juice into the bowl when he heard the tires of Jenny's big station wagon crunching on the driveway.

Jenny's mom honked the horn.

"That's Jenny, now," said A.J.'s mother. "Wipe your mouth and let's go."

"Carry me!" demanded A.J.

"Carry a big guy like you?" exclaimed A.J.'s mother. "You're much too heavy. Now come on. Jenny and her mom are waiting."

"I'm too tired." And A.J. just sat there and refused to budge.

Jenny's mom came to the door.
"Looks like it's one of those mornings," she said.
"Let me give you a hand with the baby."
"Thanks," said A.J.'s mother. "Hi, Jenny," she
called.
"Try not to be such a grouch at school, A.J.,"
his mother said. "Try to have a nice time. See
you later."

When they arrived at school Mrs. York was at
the classroom door as usual.
"Good morning, Jenny," she said. "And good
morning to you, Mr. A.J."

A.J. stomped toward his cubby dragging his backpack along the floor.

Robby stood at the cubby next to him eagerly digging into his jacket pocket.

"Look at my new key chain," Robby shouted, proudly displaying his new treasure.

"So what! That's no good!" A.J. barked. And he slammed his backpack into the cubby and stormed into the classroom.

"Yes, it is," Robby protested softly as A.J. disappeared around the corner. "My father gave it to me."

"Elizabeth, will you please choose a book and put it on my desk for today's storytime?" Mrs. York asked.

"No, it's my turn. I want to choose," A.J. whined.

A.J. turned to see Jason go riding by on a wagon.
"That's my wagon!" A.J. shouted.
"It belongs to all of us," Mrs. York reminded him.
"We always take turns."
"NO, it's mine!" complained A.J.
"You can have a turn when Jason is done."
"I can never do anything," A.J. growled.

"Let's go to the play corner," Mrs. York suggested
to A.J.
"Come on," said Elizabeth. "I'll be the mother and
you can be the baby, A.J."
A.J. obediently climbed into the stroller and started
making baby noises.
"Wah, wah," he wailed as Elizabeth pushed him
past the blocks.

"Wah, wah, wah, wah!" screamed A.J. as they drove by the fish tank.

Mrs. York and Robby were sprinkling food into the aquarium and the fish were swimming to the top of the water for breakfast.

Elizabeth walked away from the stroller and peered into the tank. She liked the bubbly noises the fish made when they slurped the food from the water.

A.J. was making such a racket that he did not notice right away that he had stopped moving.

When A.J. saw Elizabeth at the aquarium he leaped from the stroller and with one giant jump he landed at her side.
"You're supposed to be taking care of ME!" he said angrily, thumping his hands on the fish tank.
The little fish stopped eating, dove quickly to the bottom of the tank, and peered cautiously through the weeds at A.J.
"Better give the baby his bottle," said Elizabeth knowingly. "Here," she said, handing A.J. a pretend bottle. "Now go take your nap so I can feed the fish."

"YOU BE THE STUPID BABY!" yelled A.J. as he pushed Elizabeth into the stroller and bounced her across the floor.

"Where are we going?" she giggled as they raced around the room.

"To the hospital!" shouted A.J. "I'm giving this baby back."

"You can't do that," protested Elizabeth.

"Who said? Why not?" said A.J., still in a hurry.

"My mother," said Elizabeth. "And because it doesn't work that way. I tried it already when we had Jeffrey."

A.J. slowly let go of the stroller and plunked down on the floor.

Mrs. York heard their conversation.

"Is anything new at home, A.J.?" she asked.

"We have a girl baby," he said in a very small voice.

Some of the children came over to listen.

"What's her name?" Mrs. York asked.

"STUPID FACE NO NAME!" A.J. blurted out.

The other kids laughed.

"That's an unusual name," Mrs. York said. "I'll bet people make a big fuss over your new sister and you don't like that very much."

A.J. just looked down at the floor.

"They're supposed to be YOUR friends," said Mrs. York, "and when they pay attention to her it probably makes you feel pretty angry and jealous."

Just then Melissa said excitedly, "Once we took care of my cousin's puppy for a few days in our house and that's what my mother said, too. That Mitzi was . . . jealous."

"Who's Mitzi?" asked Mrs. York.

"Our dog," answered Melissa.

Some of the children giggled.

"Then what happened?" asked Mrs. York.

A.J. listened carefully.

He was very interested.

"Well, Mitzi didn't want to eat anything and she chewed up Daddy's belt and socks and she howled a lot. She even . . ."

Melissa suddenly stopped talking and looked away.

Before anyone could ask her what she was going to
say Melissa blurted out, "She even wet the floor!"
Everyone thought that was pretty funny.
They had a big laugh.
Even A.J. felt a little tickle in his chest like the
kind that makes you laugh.
But he did not laugh.

"Sometimes you want the people you love all to yourself," Mrs. York said. "We can't own another person. And that can make you feel sad sometimes. But remember, no one can own you, either. You can feel good with a lot of people. Love doesn't get used up."

"But my little brother is really okay now," offered
Elizabeth. "At first I didn't like Jeffrey because he
cried and smelled and stuff. And my mom and dad
were always watching him and doing something
with him. But now it's really neat. They let me help
and when I make faces at him he laughs even when
he's cranky."

A.J. listened, but he still was not convinced by all
the talk.

When A.J. got home from school he was still
grouchy.
In fact, he was a bigger grouch than when he went
to school in the morning.
"Did you have a nice day?" his mother asked.
A.J. shook his head silently.
"Let's have a big kiss. And how about one for the
baby?" coaxed his mother.

A.J. really did not want to, but he did it for his mother.
He gave the baby a thousand too many kisses and a hard hug.
Until she cried.
And then he walked away.
"Not so hard. Try to be more careful," warned his mother.
"You don't care about me! And Daddy doesn't care either. And all she does is cry!" A.J. snapped. "You only care about HER, HER, HER!"

"That's not true, A.J.," she said. "When Lisa falls asleep we can have some time together."
"NOW!" demanded A.J.
"All right," suggested his mother, "now you can be my helper. Maybe with your help she'll quiet down more quickly. Let's try singing a lullaby."

A.J. and his mother sang and then hummed the song together.
It made Lisa fall asleep.
Then A.J. climbed onto his mother's lap.
"Thanks for helping. She fell asleep a lot more quickly with your help," said A.J.'s mother.
"I'm a good baby. I don't cry. We don't need her anymore," he announced. "Why can't she go away?"
"I think you would like to be my one and only, like it was before," she said softly as she snuggled with him.
A.J. nestled in closer.

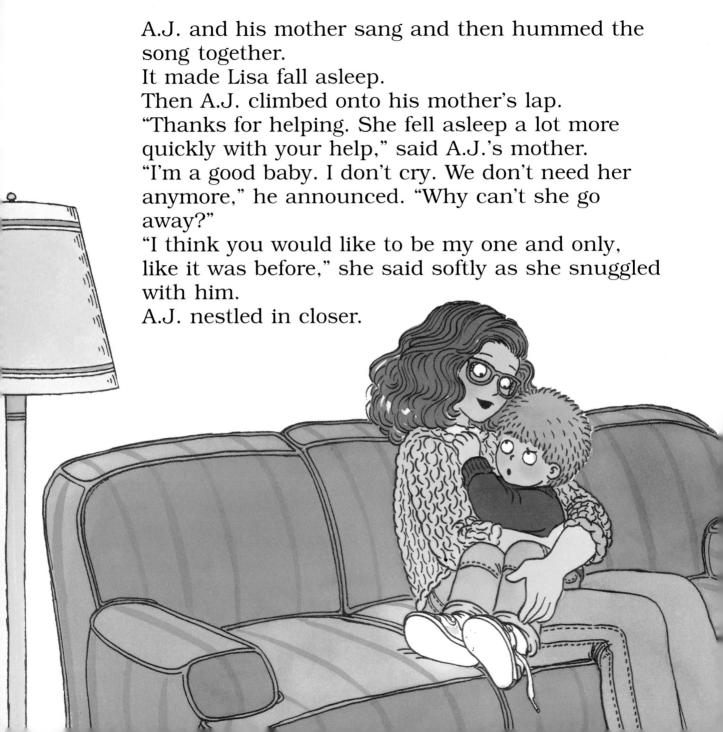

"No one can take your place. You were here first and no one else can have that special place in the family," his mother reminded him.

"She takes up too much time," A.J. complained.

"She takes up time, but she's not more important than you," his mother answered. "Besides, she has to learn a lot of things. And you can help. She can't talk. She can't eat by herself. She doesn't even know what her toes are."

A.J. smiled a little.

He felt better curled up in his mother's lap.

But later, when A.J.'s father came home the baby was crying again.
He picked up Lisa and took her into her room.
A.J. held his hands over his ears.
His father had smiled and said "Hi" when he came in, but now he was with Lisa in her room.
"Hey, A.J., come on in here," his dad called.
The baby was crying so loudly that A.J. could hardly hear his father.
"Come in so we can talk," his father repeated loudly.
"I can't talk," said A.J. "There's too much crying."

A.J. walked slowly into Lisa's room.
His father was changing her diaper.
"She certainly is noisy, isn't she?" said his father,
noticing that A.J.'s hands were still over his ears.
"Would you mind opening the new box of diapers
for me?"

"Maybe I should put my hands over my ears, too,"
his father joked.
A.J. smiled and reached for Lisa's foot.
"These are your toes, Stupid Face," he said.
And then he made the ugliest, most horrible face
anyone had ever seen.

Suddenly, she stopped crying.
She let out a little gurgle.
And then Lisa actually began to laugh.
A.J. and his father were so surprised that they started to laugh, too.
Hearing all the laughter, A.J.'s mother came to Lisa's room.
It was the first time that Lisa had ever laughed like that.
"A.J., you're going to be a terrific big brother," praised his mother.
And for the first time that day A.J. felt REALLY SPECIAL.

Later that night, after the sun had gone down, A.J. remembered what Elizabeth had said.
"Maybe having a baby sister would be really neat— well, maybe sometimes!" he thought.
And he settled into a sound sleep.
It was going to be a peaceful night in Crescent Canyon. . . if only Lisa would stay asleep, too.